The Magic Porridge Pot

BY PAUL GALDONE

A CLARION BOOK / THE SEABURY PRESS
NEW YORK

for Phoebe

The Seabury Press, 815 Second Avenue, New York, N.Y. 10017

Copyright © 1976 by Paul Galdone
Printed in the United States of America

Library of Congress Cataloging in Publication Data

Galdone, Paul.   The magic porridge pot.
"A Clarion book."
SUMMARY: The porridge pot always produces food for the little
girl, but it runs amuck when her mother tries to use it without
knowing the magic words to stop it.
[1. Magic—Fiction]   I. Title.
PZ7.G1305Mag   [E]   76-3531   ISBN 0-8164-3173-6

Once upon a time, long, long ago,
a little girl and her mother lived in a small cottage
at the end of the village street.
They were so poor that often
there was nothing to eat in the house
but a small piece of bread.

When their cupboard was bare,
the little girl would go into the forest
near the cottage to search for nuts and berries.
One chilly morning she wandered
through the dark forest,
but she could not find a single nut or berry.

At last the little girl sat down on a fallen tree
and started to cry.
"There's no food for Mother and me.
What will we do? We're so hungry."
"Cheer up, my dear," said a pleasant but crackly voice.
The little girl looked up in surprise
to see an old woman who wore
a long cloak and leaned on a crooked stick.

"Do not worry, my dear," said the old woman.
"You need never be hungry again."
From under her cloak she drew out a small black pot.
"This is a magic pot, my dear.
After you put it on the fire, you must say to it,
    'Boil, Little Pot, boil!'
and at once it will fill up with delicious porridge.
When you have had all you can eat, you must say to it,
    'Stop, Little Pot, stop!'
and the magic pot will stop boiling."
"Oh, thank you so much," said the little girl.
"Never forget the magic words, my dear,"
said the old woman. "Never forget!"
And no sooner had she said this
than she vanished.

The little girl carried the pot home
as fast as she could run through the forest.

"What have you there?" her mother asked.

"This is a magic pot that will cook
  delicious porridge," the little girl explained.
"An old woman gave it to me in the forest."

The little girl was eager to try out the magic pot.
She set it on the fire and said,
"Boil, Little Pot, boil!"

Sure enough, delicious porridge bubbled up.

When they had had all that they could eat,
the little girl said,
"Stop, Little Pot, stop!"

and the magic pot stopped boiling.

For a long time the little girl and her mother
had as much porridge as they wanted,
and were very happy and contented.

Then one day the little girl decided to visit
her friend at the other end of the village.

The little girl was gone a long while
and her mother began to be hungry.
So she set the magic pot on the fire and said to it,
    "Boil, Little Pot, boil!"
The porridge began to rise in the pot,
and the mother dished out a nice bowlful.

Soon the porridge was bubbling at the top of the pot.
But the mother had forgotten the magic words!

    The porridge kept on rising

    and began to spill over the rim.

    "Halt, Little Pot, halt!" the mother said.

The porridge only boiled
and bubbled over faster.
"Enough, Little Pot, enough!"
cried the mother, trying to remember
the right words.
The porridge flowed down until
it covered the floor of the cottage.

The mother struggled to the door
and opened it wide to let the porridge
flow out of the house.
"No more, Little Pot, no more," she shouted.

The stream of delicious porridge flowed
through the cottage door and onto the street.
Down the street ran the mother screaming,
"Cease, Little Pot, cease!"
But the porridge flowed on and on,
toward the very last house in the village
where the little girl was visiting.

When the mother reached the house she called,
"Help, help! The magic pot keeps boiling, boiling, boiling!"

At once the little girl guessed what was wrong.
So she waded into the thick, heavy porridge and ran home
as fast as she could, with her mother behind her.

When the little girl reached the cottage she cried,
"Stop, Little Pot, stop!
Stop, Little Pot, stop!
Stop, Little Pot, stop!
Stop, Little Pot, stop!"
And the magic pot stopped boiling.

Then everyone in the village came out into the street
carrying dippers, spoons, cups, bowls, buckets,
platters, pans, plates, and pitchers.
They dipped up the porridge and they scooped
up the porridge, and they spooned up the porridge.
There was enough porridge for everyone
to feast on for days and days.

After that, the little girl and her mother
and the people of the village never
went hungry. But they never forgot
the words to stop the magic pot from boiling.

"Stop, Little Pot, stop!"